For all the ones we really miss.

—Patrick and Jonathan

First published in 2020 by Little Hare Books
an imprint of Hardie Grant Egmont
Ground Floor, Building 1, 658 Church Street
Richmond, Victoria 3121, Australia

This 2020 edition published by Starry Forest Books, Inc.
Starry Forest® is a registered trademark of Starry Forest Books, Inc.
P.O. Box 1797, 217 East 70th Street, New York, NY 10021

ISBN 978-1-946000-64-4

Manufactured in China

Lot #: 2 4 6 8 10 9 7 5 3 1

10/20

WINDOWS

PATRICK GUEST

JONATHAN BENTLEY

Starry Forest Books

Out the window, I can see
a new world looking back at me.

The streets are still,
there are no crowds …

but looking up, I see the clouds.

There goes one that's bringing rain.
There goes one like an old steam train.

A pirate ship goes sailing by,
a dinosaur fills half the sky.

We can all look up and watch the weather,
even though we're not together.

What is that I hear below?
It's a friendly nurse saying hello.

And look, my friends are out there too!
I can see Mikayla and Abu.

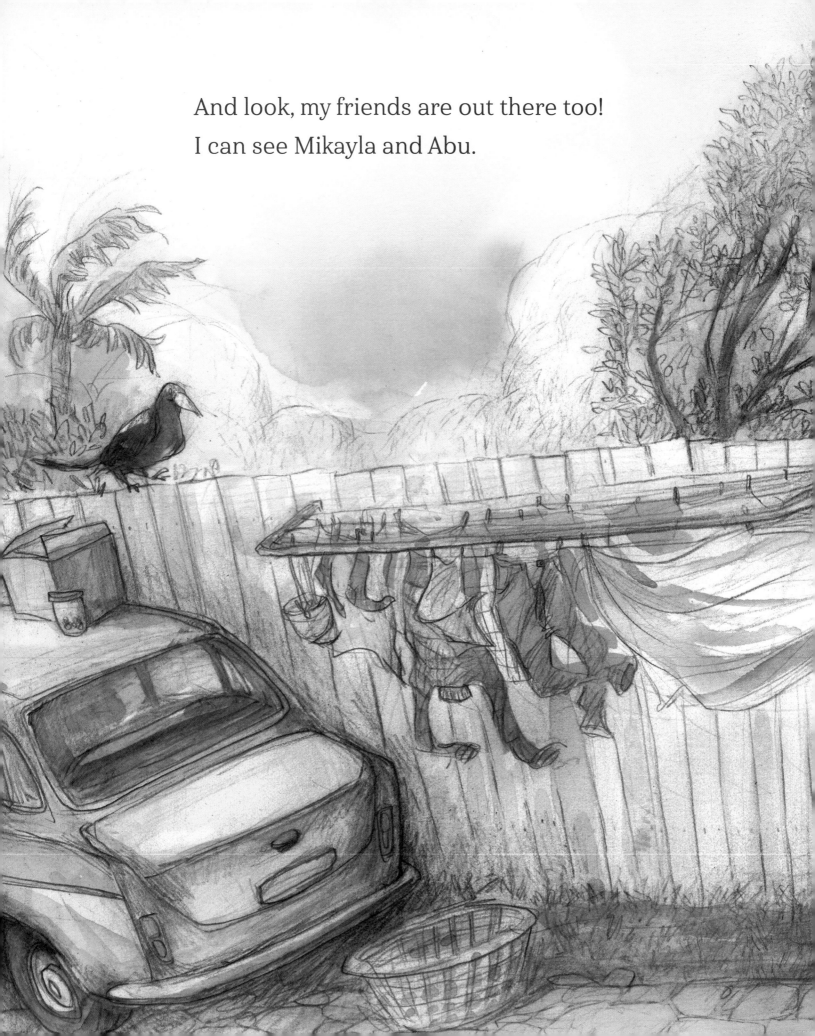

A fire truck gives me a toot,
Giuseppe's Mamma plays the flute.

Kiyoshi smiles
and waves his coat,

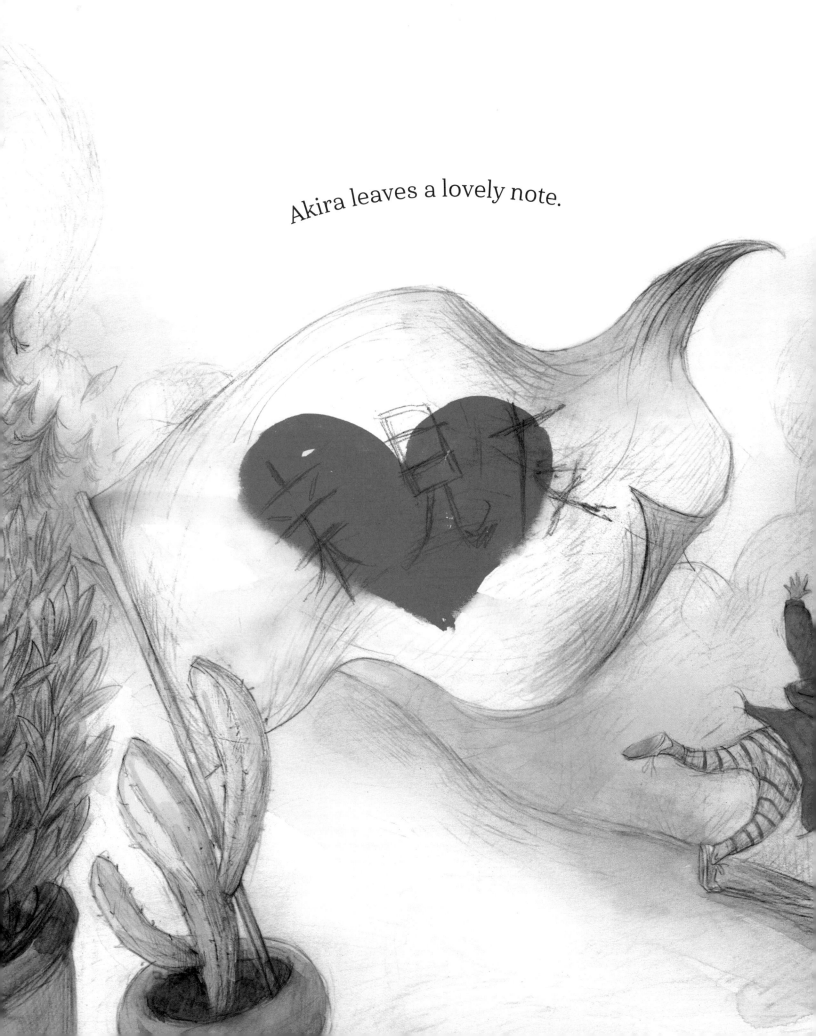

Akira leaves a lovely note.

In different windows everywhere,

I see rainbows, hearts, and teddy bears.

What's that tapping on the glass?
Is it a ghost, just floating past?

And what's that flying
thing I see?

Is that a hat?
Whose could it be?

I think I'd better close the curtain
until I know I'm safe, for certain.

But when I pull
the curtain away . . .

I see my Grandpa and shout,

"HOORAY!"

He pulls a face
and does a **jig,**

he blows and makes
his mouth look **BIG.**

He flaps his arms,
pretends they're **wings,**

then he smiles at me and **sings:**

"I'd love to give you all a **hug,**

I'd love to squash this silly **bug,**

but just for now I'll keep **away**,

until the lovely, happy **day**

when all the world can dance and kiss . . .

and hug the ones
we really miss."